THIS LITTLE TIGER BOOK BELONGS TO:

_____

_____

_____

_____

The Very Noisy Night

Diana Hendry   Jane Chapman

LITTLE TIGER PRESS
London

It was the middle of the
night, and Big Mouse was
fast asleep in his big bed.
Little Mouse was wide
awake in his little bed.
"Big Mouse! Big Mouse!"
called Little Mouse.
"I can hear something
rushing round the house,
huffing and puffing."

Big Mouse opened one eye and one ear.
"It's only the wind," he said.

"Can I come into your bed?" asked Little Mouse.
"No," said Big Mouse. "There isn't room."
And he turned over and went back to sleep.

Little Mouse lay listening to the wind. Then, suddenly, between a huff and a puff, came a . . .

TAP TAP TAP

TAP

Little Mouse climbed out of bed, opened the front door — just a crack — and peeped out.

WHOOOSH!

went the wind, but there was no one outside. "Big Mouse! Big Mouse!" called Little Mouse. "I can hear someone tapping. Perhaps there's a burglar on the roof."

Big Mouse got out of
bed and opened the bedroom
curtains. "Look," he said, "it's
only a branch tapping on the
window. Go back to sleep."
   "Can I come into your bed?"
asked Little Mouse.
   "No," said Big Mouse.
"You wriggle."

Little Mouse lay in his
own bed and listened
to the wind huffing
and puffing and the
branch tap-tapping —
and someone calling,

"HOO-HOO!
HOO-HOO!"

Little Mouse climbed out of bed again. This time he looked under it. Then he looked in the wardrobe, and feeling very frightened he cried, "Big Mouse! Big Mouse! I think there's a ghost in the house, and it's looking for me. It keeps calling, who who? who who?"

Big Mouse sighed, sat up
and listened. "It's only an owl,"
he said. "It's awake, like you."
"Can I come into your bed?"
asked Little Mouse.
"No," said Big Mouse. "Your
paws are always cold."
And Big Mouse pulled the
blanket over his head and
went back to sleep.

Little Mouse got back into his own bed and he lay and listened to the wind huffing and puffing, the branch tap-tapping, and the owl hooting. But sssh! What was that?

CARPET

3

DRIP DRIP DRIP

DRIP

"Big Mouse! Big Mouse!" he called. "I think it's raining inside." And Little Mouse jumped out of bed and fetched his red umbrella.

Big Mouse got out of bed too. He opened the front door. "Be quiet, wind," he said. "Be quiet, branch. Be quiet, owl." But they took no notice. Then Big Mouse went into the kitchen, turned off the dripping tap and put away the umbrella.

"Can I come into your bed?"
asked Little Mouse.
   "No, you're nice and snug in your own bed,"
said Big Mouse, taking him back to the bedroom.

Little Mouse lay and listened
to the wind huffing and
puffing, the branch tap-tapping,
and the owl hooting.
And just as he was beginning
to feel very sleepy indeed,
he heard . . .

"WhEEE,
WHEEE,
WHEEEEE!"

"Big Mouse! Big Mouse!"
he called. "You're snoring."

Wearily Big Mouse got up. He put his ear-muffs on Little Mouse's ears. He put a paper-clip on his own nose, and he went back to bed.

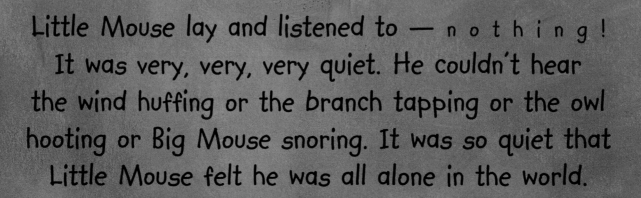

Little Mouse lay and listened to — n o t h i n g !
It was very, very, very quiet. He couldn't hear
the wind huffing or the branch tapping or the owl
hooting or Big Mouse snoring. It was so quiet that
Little Mouse felt he was all alone in the world.

He took off the ear-muffs.
He got out of bed and pulled the paper-clip
off Big Mouse's nose. "Big Mouse! Big Mouse!"
he cried, "I'm lonely!"

Big Mouse flung back
his blanket. "Better come
into my bed," he said.
So Little Mouse hopped
in and his paws
were cold...

and he needed just
a little wriggle before
he fell fast asleep.

Big Mouse lay and listened to the wind
huffing and puffing and the branch
tapping and the owl hooting and
Little Mouse snuffling, and very
soon he heard the birds
waking up. But neither
of them heard the
alarm clock...

... BECAUSE THEY WERE
BOTH FAST ASLEEP!

For Emelia, with love
— D H

For Anthony, Jane, Mark,
Katy and Alice, with love
— J C

LITTLE TIGER PRESS
1 The Coda Centre, 189 Munster Road, London SW6 6AW
www.littletiger.co.uk
First published in Great Britain 1999 • This edition published 2016
Text copyright © Diana Hendry 1999 • Illustrations copyright © Jane Chapman 1999
Visit Jane Chapman at www.ChapmanandWarnes.com
Diana Hendry and Jane Chapman have asserted their rights to be
identified as the author and illustrator of this work under the
Copyright, Designs and Patents Act, 1988.
All rights reserved • ISBN 978-1-84869-386-9
Printed in China • LTP/1900/1740/1216
3 5 7 9 10 8 6 4 2

CD track 1 – complete story with original music and sound effects
CD track 2 – story with page turn pings encourages learner readers to join in

Running time – over 15 mins • Produced by The Complete Works, Warwickshire CV31 1JP,
in conjunction with Stationhouse • Music composed by Jim Betteridge and Sam Park

Visit our website www.littletiger.co.uk for details of other Little Tiger Picture Book
and CD Sets, plus our full catalogue of novelty, board and picture books.